goggi-geeha ...

EGMONT

We bring stories to life

First published in Great Britain 2012 by Egmont UK Limited
239 Kensington High Street, London W8 6SA

Baby Jake characters and logo © Darrall Macqueen Limited
2012. Baby Jake is a trademark of Darrall Macqueen
Limited. Licensed by BBC Worldwide Limited.
BBC logo TM & © BBC 1996. All rights reserved.

BBC | **Darrall Macqueen** LTD

ISBN 978 1 4052 6365 8
51918/1
Printed in Italy

It's time for an ADVENTURE,

Baby Jake

TROPICAL
Adventure

Look! A palm tree!

Palm trees everywhere.

Get ready for a **tropical** adventure - yippee!

Hello, Baby Jake.

You are very giggly today!

Is someone tickling your toes?

Yes, it's Sydney the Monkey.

Hello, Sydney.

Baby Jake loves tickle toes,

Tickle toes wherever he goes!

Ooo-ooo-ooo!

Wow!

Look at you, Baby Jake!

Clack, clack, clackerty clack!

The trees are clacking their coconuts!

You're clacking coconuts too, Jakey!

That does look fun!

Boogie-woogie, tip-tappy,

happy clappy Baby Jake.

Baby Jake wants to sing with you –
You know the words,
you used to sing them too ...

Yacki, yacki, yoggi – doo, doo, dee.
Bah, bah, bah, beep beep – noo see!
Yacki, yacki, yoggi – moo moo moo.
That's just what we love to do!

Yacki, yacki, yoggi,
let's do it **again!**

Yacki, yacki, yoggi – doo, doo, dee.
Yacki, yacki, yoggi, beep beep – noo see!
Bah, bah, bah, beep beep – noo see!
Yacki, yacki, yoggi – moo moo moo.
That's just what we love to do!

Yacki, yacki, yoggi – doo, doo, dee.
Bah, bah, bah, beep beep – noo see!
Yacki, yacki, yoggi – moo moo moo.
Hope you love to do it too!

Baby Jake you are the boogie best.

What are you doing now, Jakey?

Wheeeeeee!

Wheeeeeee!

Baby Jake is tree sliding

with Sydney!

Look at that, Baby Jake!

It's a vine!

A sparkly vine hanging from a tree.

Oh, no. You're not going to, are you Baby Jake?

You are!

Baby Jake is swinging through the trees on a vine!

Baby Jake is swinging all the way home!

Wheeeeeee!

Bye bye **Sydney!**

Bye bye **clickety, clackerty coconuts!**

Bye bye **palm trees!**

Goodbye!

Baby Jake and me,
Baby Jake and you,

We've had a **MAGIC** time today...

Dee zee dee see doo!